IT'S THE TOP OF THE LAST INNING—AND THE NEVER SINK NINE IS BEHIND BY A RUN

Pete was on second base with two out.

Mike slipped on his batting gloves and grabbed a bat. He started for the plate.

"Hey, Mike," said Otis, "if you hit Pete home, you'll tie the game."

Jenny tugged on Walter's sleeve. She pointed toward Pete on second base. He was squeezing the second baseman's nose. Pennies dropped to the ground. The Never Sink Nine was depending on Pete and he was doing magic tricks!

"Pete!" shouted Walter.

Pete waved at Walter and went back to his penny trick.

Mike hammered a grounder past the pitcher straight to second base. The second baseman was busy with Pete's penny trick! He wasn't even looking. Pete raced for third. His magic was working!

Other Bantam Skylark Books you will enjoy
Ask your bookseller for the books you have
  missed

THE NEVER SINK NINE

Pete the Magnificent

BY GIBBS DAVIS

Illustrated by
George Ulrich

A BANTAM SKYLARK BOOK©
NEW YORK • TORONTO • LONDON • SYDNEY • AUCKLAND

RL 2, 005–008

PETE THE MAGNIFICENT
A Bantam Skylark Book / June 1991

*Skylark Books is a registered trademark of Bantam Books, a division
of Bantam Doubleday Dell Publishing Group, Inc. Registered in
U.S. Patent and Trademark Office and elsewhere.*

ISBN 0-553-15896-1

Published simultaneously in the United States and Canada

*Bantam Books are published by Bantam Books, a division of Bantam Double-
day Dell Publishing Group, Inc. Its trademark, consisting of the words
"Bantam Books" and the portrayal of a rooster, is Registered in U.S. Patent
and Trademark Office and in other countries. Marca Registrada. Bantam
Books, 666 Fifth Avenue, New York, New York 10103.*

PRINTED IN THE UNITED STATES OF AMERICA

CWO   0 9 8 7 6 5 4 3 2 1

In memory of my grandfather, "Pum Pum,"
who put himself through college
playing semiprofessional baseball
in the 1890s

CHAPTER ONE

Pete's Joke of the Day

Walter Dodd raced down the hall of Eleanor Roosevelt Elementary and burst into Mrs. Howard's third grade classroom. He plowed down the aisle to his desk and pulled a small book out of his backpack: *The Pitcher's Guide*.

It was Wednesday. In three days Walter would be pitching his first game for his baseball team, the Never Sink Nine.

Walter checked his official Babe Ruth wristwatch. Five minutes until school started. He flipped through the section on catcher's signals. There were a zillion of them.

1

"I'll never learn them in time," muttered Walter. He closed his eyes and tried to remember the signal for a fastball.

"Hey, Walt, what's up?" asked a boy across the aisle. It was Mike Lasky, Walter's best friend. Mike played shortstop for the Never Sink Nine. Right now he was chewing a big wad of gum.

Walter didn't answer. He squeezed his eyes tighter and tried to see the signal for a curve ball.

"What are you looking at?" Mike leaned across the aisle to see. He blew a big pink bubble in Walter's face.

"Nothing," Walter grumbled, pulling his book away.

Mike stared at his friend.

Walter felt bad. He never kept secrets from Mike. "What if I bomb this Saturday?" he whispered.

Mike's face softened. "Don't worry. You'll be okay."

"Easy for you to say." Mike was already good at hitting. Walter wanted to be really good at something, too. *I have to be a good pitcher,* he thought.

"Whoa, Melissa," Mike said. A girl in cowboy boots was prancing down the aisle like a pony.

Walter rolled his eyes at Mike. Melissa Nichols was the horse-craziest girl in school. She was also the best pitcher the Never Sink Nine had. Walter quickly hid his book. He didn't want Melissa to know he was worried.

Melissa set down her backpack on her desk. She started pulling toy horses out of it, one at a time. Suddenly she stopped and squinched up her nose. "P.U.!" she said. "Something smells bad!" She sniffed around Walter's desk. "Walter, are you wearing those stinko socks of yours again?"

Walter's ears started to burn. "Those are my *lucky* socks and any turkey brain knows you can't wash them or the luck comes out." His grandfather, Grandpa Walt, had given them to him at the start of the baseball season. Walter hadn't washed them once.

Melissa rolled her eyes in disgust.

Walter shoved up his sleeve. His arm was

shiny. "For your information that smell is Tiger Balm. All the pros use it on their pitching arm."

Melissa tossed her long red hair back like a horse's mane. "Just because you're pitching *half* a game with me this Saturday, don't get used to it."

"You don't own the mound," said Walter.

"Yeah," said Mike, backing up his friend.

Melissa ignored them.

Walter was memorizing the signal for a change-up when Mike leaned over and jabbed him in the arm.

"Look at the board," he whispered.

"I'm busy," said Walter. Didn't anyone realize pitching was serious business?

"You'd better look," said Mike.

Walter closed his book and looked at the blackboard. A tall boy with curly dark hair was writing on it. Pete Santos had moved to Rockville last week. He was the newest member of the Never Sink Nine, and his pet goat, Homer, was the team's new mascot. Every day Pete wrote a new joke on the board before Mrs. Howard came to class.

Walter read today's joke:

4

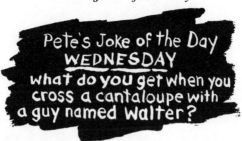

Walter's ears tingled. Everyone was giggling and looking at him.

Walter stood up. "Hey, what's the big idea, Santos?"

"Lighten up, Dodd," said Christy Chung. "Not everyone gets to be joke of the day."

"Where's the answer?" Mike asked Pete. Pete left the answer to his joke in a different place every day.

"Yeah, Pete," begged Melissa. "Tell us where you put it."

Pete strutted up and down the aisle with a big grin on his face.

"Show-off," said Walter. Pete Santos had been in their class for hardly more than a week and he was getting more attention than Walter got in his whole life. It wasn't fair.

"Okay, sports fans," said Pete. "The answer to today's joke is . . ."

5

Everyone leaned forward to hear, including Walter.

"... on the playground under the jungle gym."

A handful of students started for the playground. Just as they reached the door, Mrs. Howard appeared. As usual, their teacher wore a flowered dress. Big plastic daisy earrings dangled from her ears.

"What's going on here?" asked Mrs. Howard.

Everyone walked back to their desks.

Mrs. Howard looked up at Pete's joke on the blackboard. "Okay, Pete. Where's the answer to to-day's joke?"

Pete blushed. "Under the jungle gym."

"You'll just have to wait until recess to find out the punchline," Mrs. Howard said. She hid a smile as she turned and wrote PARENTS' NIGHT on the blackboard.

Walter couldn't believe it. Mrs. Howard didn't even erase Pete's joke.

"This Friday is Parents' Night," said Mrs. Howard. "Some of you have worked very hard on the talent show, but not everyone has signed up.

7

We *all* have to contribute to the night's fun." Mrs. Howard looked at Walter.

Walter slid down in his chair. How could he think of Parents' Night when he had Saturday's game to worry about?

"Not all of us can play the piano like Mike or draw like Tony," said Mrs. Howard. "But everyone can read a poem or sing a song."

Pete raised his hand.

"Yes, Pete," said Mrs. Howard.

"Can I bring Homer to school on Parents' Night?"

"Why do you want to bring your pet goat to school?" Mrs. Howard asked.

"He's part of my magic act," said Pete.

"No goats allowed," said Mrs. Howard.

"Okay," said Pete. "Homer's favorite TV show is on Friday night anyway. He wouldn't want to miss it."

A wave of giggles went across the room.

"Settle down, everyone," said Mrs. Howard. "It's time for math to begin."

Mike rolled a pencil off his desk. He leaned over to pick it up and looked at Walter. It was their new secret signal to meet in the bathroom.

Mike raised his hand. "I have to go to the bathroom."

Mrs. Howard nodded and Mike left the room.

Exactly two minutes later Walter raised his hand.

"Go on, Walter," said Mrs. Howard. "But I want you and Mike back at your desks in five minutes."

Walter found Mike waiting for him outside the classroom door.

"Come on," whispered Mike, leading the way down the hall.

Walter followed his friend out the door to the playground. They made a dash for the jungle gym. Mike got there first.

"Over there," said Mike, pointing to a word written in chalk on the asphalt.

Walter climbed inside the jungle gym. Pete's joke went through his head. *What do you get when you cross a cantaloupe with a guy named Walter?* He stood above the answer and read it out loud.

"A Waltermelon," he said, and frowned.

Mike bent over laughing. "That's great," he said. "A *Walter*melon!"

9

Walter looked at his friend. "I don't think it's so funny."

Mike straightened up. Tears of laughter trickled down his face.

A large, round-faced boy jogged toward them across the playground. "Otis Hooper," said Walter. "What's *he* doing out here?"

Otis leaned against the jungle gym and tried to catch his breath.

"Couldn't wait until recess either, could you?" said Mike. "The answer's a Waltermelon."

Otis chuckled. "That's a good one," he said. "Mrs. Howard sent me to get you."

"Uh, oh," said Mike.

Walter looked up at the class window. Mrs. Howard was looking right back at him! Walter waved weakly at her. Mrs. Howard didn't wave back.

"She said if you two like being outside so much you can weed the class garden after school today." Otis grinned.

Walter and Mike each let out a long groan.

"We'd better go," said Mike, heading back.

Walter started after him.

"Hey, Walter," said Otis. "I hear you're pitching on Saturday."

"Yeah." Walter knew he'd be pitching to Otis at the game. Otis was the Never Sink Nine's catcher.

Otis walked alongside Walter. "Are you scared?" He looked at Walter closely.

"No," lied Walter. "Why?"

"Because we've won three games in a row," said Otis. "If you mess up you'll wreck everything."

Walter's heart sank. He looked at their classroom window. Mrs. Howard was still looking at him. And she still wasn't smiling.

There were only two days until Parents' Night and three days until the game.

Walter wasn't ready for either one.

CHAPTER TWO

Glass-Arm
Pitcher

After school on Thursday Walter and Mike bicycled toward Diamond Park for team practice.

A woman was standing in the intersection. She wore a bright orange vest and white gloves. Mrs. Miller had been the crossing guard since Walter was in kindergarten.

Walter looked at Diamond Park's three baseball fields across the street. They were filling up fast. Walter rolled his bike to the edge of the curb.

"Which team are you boys on?" Mrs. Miller asked. "Polar Blasts? The Drill Team?"

13

"We beat them both already," said Mike. "We're the Never Sink Nine."

"We've won all our games," added Walter.

Walter and Mike smiled at each other.

"You boys sound tough," said Mrs. Miller. "Who'll you beat this week?"

"The Bug Busters," said Walter.

"Watch out for the Decker twins." Mrs. Miller walked into the street with her stop sign held high. She waved them on. "Good luck!" she yelled after them.

Walter pedaled up next to Mike. "Who're the Decker twins?"

"Only the best pitchers in the Rockville League," said Mike.

Suddenly Walter's legs felt weak. *What if I lose Saturday's game and let everyone down?* he thought. He coasted slowly onto Mickey Mantle field. The Never Sink Nine was warming up.

At the dugout everyone was talking about Pete's joke of the day.

Melissa Nichols' younger sister, Jenny, tugged on Walter's sleeve. "What was the joke?" she asked. "No one will tell me." Jenny was the youngest member of the Never Sink Nine.

14

"Ask someone else," said Walter. He was sick of Pete and his jokes.

Jenny looked as if she might cry.

"Okay, okay," said Walter. "What has eighteen legs and catches flies?"

Jenny tugged on one of her braids. "Umm, two spiders?"

Walter shook his head. "A baseball team."

Jenny frowned. "I don't get it."

Walter sighed. "A baseball team has nine players. Each player has two legs. That's eighteen legs." He lifted his mitt in the air and pretended to catch a fly ball. "And we catch flies. Now do you get it?"

A slow smile spread across Jenny's face. "That's funny."

Suddenly a loud whistle blew. Grandpa Walt, the Never Sink Nine coach, was waving everyone onto the field.

"Come on," Walter said to Jenny. "Practice is starting."

Walter was proud of his grandfather. Grandpa Walt was the only coach in the Rockville League who had played in the minors.

Jenny followed Walter onto the field.

15

"Okay, team," said Grandpa Walt. "Did everyone practice catching fly balls this week?"

A few heads nodded.

Walter rubbed his sore arm. The only thing he'd practiced was pitching.

"Good," said Grandpa Walt. "We've got a tough game coming up on Saturday. The Bug Busters haven't lost any games either."

"Ba-a-a-a! Ba-a-a-a!"

Everyone turned. Pete Santos and his pet goat, Homer, were walking across the field. Homer was wearing his Never Sink Nine baseball cap. Pete was carrying a jar in his hand.

"Sorry I'm late, Coach," said Pete. "I had to feed the team mascot and get this." He handed the jar to Grandpa Walt.

Walter moved closer to see what was inside the jar. It looked like a bunch of flies.

"What's this for?" asked Grandpa Walt.

"You told us to go home and practice catching flies," said Pete. "Here's a jar full and I caught every one of them."

Everyone looked up at Grandpa Walt to see what he would do. Walter held his breath.

16

Grandpa Walt grinned. Then he smiled. Then he exploded into laughter.

Walter looked around. The whole Never Sink Nine was laughing! Even Homer was wagging his tail.

Otis poked Walter in the ribs. "What's wrong? Someone steal your funny bone?"

"Yeah," said Melissa. "You've been a real sourpuss lately."

"He's scared about pitching Saturday," whispered Otis.

"I am not!" said Walter. He wanted to punch Otis in the face.

Grandpa Walt put a hand on Walter's shoulder. "*All* of you are going to be trying out new positions sometime during the season. This Saturday it will be Pete, Melissa, and Walter."

Walter hadn't thought about anyone else having to play a new position. Pete already took Billy Baskin's old place on first. Billy Baskin had been the team slugger before he moved away.

"Everyone take the field, except Walter!" said Grandpa Walt. "I'm hitting fly balls and I want to see everyone's mitt in the air!"

17

Walter waited to be told what to do. He watched Grandpa Walt pick up a bat and walk over to home plate.

"What're you waiting for?" Grandpa Walt asked him. "I can't hit without a pitcher."

Suddenly Walter realized *he* was the pitcher. He jogged up to the mound and fired the first ball with all his might.

Grandpa Walt watched as it sailed over his head. "Don't throw so hard," he said. "Just get it in the strike zone."

Walter knew that meant between Grandpa Walt's shoulders and knees. He managed to get the next one over the plate.

Grandpa Walt swung his bat.

Pop!

A perfect fly ball! Walter watched the ball sail over his head.

"I've got it!" yelled Katie Kessler on third. She backed into the outfield.

"It's mine!" Felix Smith yelled, squinting into the sun.

"Look out!" Jenny charged the ball.

Katie, Felix, and Jenny all tried to get under the ball.

19

Walter couldn't look. He hid his face behind his mitt.

"Oof!"

"Ouch!"

Walter peered over his mitt. Katie, Felix, and Jenny were piled on top of one another. The ball rolled to a stop a few feet away.

Grandpa Walt jogged into the outfield to make sure everyone was okay. "Good try," he said, helping Jenny up. "All you need are a few pointers."

Grandpa Walt showed them how to use both hands to make a catch. "Soon as the ball hits the pocket, cover it with your free hand," he said. "Otherwise it might fall out."

After a few tries everyone was getting the hang of it.

Walter's arm was already tired. He wound up and threw a wild pitch that landed in the bleachers.

"You look like a glass-arm pitcher!" someone shouted from the sidelines.

Walter looked over at a freckle-faced boy. He wore a Bug Busters T-shirt. Walter started to ignore him, and turned away.

"He'll never make it through a game!" shouted someone else

Walter turned to see an *identical* freckle-faced boy standing beside the first one. "The Decker twins," he said to himself. Their T-shirts read:

RIZZO'S BUG BUSTERS
Bug Off!

Grandpa Walt dropped his bat and walked straight over to the Decker twins. They looked scared. Walter had forgotten how big and powerful his grandfather could look. When Grandpa Walt stopped talking the boys ran off the field.

"I think everyone's getting a little tired," Grandpa Walt said to the team. "Let's call it a day. I'll see you all on the Babe Ruth field Saturday morning. We play the Bug Busters at ten A.M. sharp."

The Never Sink Nine headed back to the dugout.

Walter jogged over to Otis. "I need some help with catcher's signals," he said. "Wanna stay and practice?"

"No way," said Otis, walking off. "I'm beat."

21

Walter turned to Mike. "Let's hit a few," he said.

"Can't," said Mike. He stuffed his mitt in his backpack and swung it over his shoulder. "Gotta practice for Parents' Night. My dad's gonna be there. He said I better be good after all the piano lessons he's paid for."

Walter felt desperate. Everyone was deserting him. Christy Chung was the only one left in the dugout. She was putting on her pink ballet slippers.

"I need some more practice," pleaded Walter. "Wanna—"

"Forget it, Walter," said Christy. "I'm working on my dance for Parents' Night." She held her arms over her head. "I'll be a maple leaf. What are you gonna do?"

"It's a surprise," said Walter, turning away. His face always got red when he lied. *Grandpa Walt's my only hope*, he thought. *He won't let me down.*

Grandpa Walt leaned into the dugout. "Walter, will you help Pete collect the bases and return the equipment bag? I've got a dentist appointment and I'm running late."

Walter climbed out of the dugout with the equipment bag.

Homer was eating grass near first base. Walter went over and rubbed the goat's long furry ears. "I don't suppose *you* could help me out," he said.

A fly landed on Homer's nose. He shook his head back and forth.

"So you won't help either," said Walter, feeling more and more sorry for himself.

Walter picked up first base and dropped it into the equipment bag. "Bet Babe Ruth never had to clean up after a game," he said to Homer.

CHAPTER THREE

Pitching Is Serious Business

Walter dragged the equipment bag across Diamond Park. It felt like a ton of bricks instead of a few bats and bases.

"Hey, Walter, wait up!" Pete and Homer were running after him. "We're supposed to do this together!"

"I don't have time for jokes," said Walter. He stopped to catch his breath.

Pete quickly tied the equipment bag to Homer's collar. "Come on, Homer," he said, walking ahead of the goat. "We need help." Homer followed Pete, dragging the bag slowly.

"See," said Pete. "Things don't have to be hard."

"I didn't know goats were so strong," said Walter.

"They're smart, too," said Pete. "Smarter than dogs. Homer talks to me all the time."

"Sure," said Walter. "I'll bet he reads the paper too."

"Sometimes," said Pete, thoughtfully. "Mostly the funnies." He opened the door to the equipment shed. Homer dragged the bag inside.

Homer nuzzled Pete's jacket pocket.

"Okay, okay," said Pete, reaching into his pocket. He pulled out an apple. Homer grabbed it with his strong teeth.

"I gotta go," said Walter, walking away.

"Isn't your brother first baseman for the Flyers?" Pete called after him.

"Yeah," said Walter, getting on his bike.

"Think he'd give me some pointers?" Pete asked.

"Danny's in the fourth grade," said Walter. "He doesn't talk to third-graders."

"Ever?" asked Pete.

"You can try." Walter pushed off on his bike.

27

"Where do you live?" Pete asked quickly.

Walter shouted over his shoulder, "Elm Street!"

Walter pedaled across Diamond Park laughing to himself. His big brother Danny never spoke to any of Walter's friends. He called them babies. Boy, was Pete in for a surprise!

As soon as Walter got home he ran up to his room and got out *The Pitcher's Guide*. Walter checked his Babe Ruth watch. One hour until dinner. Enough time to read Chapter Four—The Windup.

Walter was halfway through the chapter when he heard Danny laughing under his window. Someone was laughing with him.

"Be quiet!" shouted Walter. "I'm trying to read!" He walked to the window and looked down to see who was making all the noise.

Walter couldn't believe his eyes. It was his big brother Danny with Pete!

Danny shouted up to Walter, "Why didn't you tell me you had a friend who does magic tricks?"

Pete waved at Walter.

"You gotta see this trick," Danny said, excited. "Come on down!"

Walter pulled his head in from the window. What was going on? He raced downstairs and opened the front door. Homer was chewing Mrs. Dodd's lilac bushes.

Pete was pretending to squeeze pennies from Danny's nose. Five copper pennies dropped from Danny's nose.

Danny burst out laughing. "How'd you do it?" he begged Pete.

Walter stood frozen in the doorway. Danny was treating Pete like a fourth-grader!

Danny took Walter by the arm and pulled him into the yard. "Do that watch trick on Walt," he said to Pete.

Pete nodded and held up his bare wrist for Walter to see. "I don't have a watch. Can I borrow yours?"

Walter shoved his hands deep into his pockets. He *loved* his new official Babe Ruth watch. It took months of eating Mrs. Olsen's Oat Bran cereal to collect enough box tops to get it. Walter didn't even take it off in the shower.

He just stuck his arm outside the shower curtain.

"No," said Walter. "Do a different trick."

"Don't be a jerk," said Danny. "Give him your watch."

Walter slowly took off his watch and handed it over to Pete.

Pete held the watch up to his ear and shook his head. "It's not ticking," he said. "I'll fix it."

Pete switched the watch to his other hand. He raised his arm and threw the watch down onto the driveway! It smashed into a dozen pieces.

"My watch!" shouted Walter. "You broke it!" He lunged at Pete.

Danny pulled Walter off of Pete.

Walter squirmed to get away. "Let me go!" yelled Walter. "I'm gonna kill him!"

"Hold on," Danny laughed. "Show him, Pete."

Pete opened his other hand. Inside was Walter's watch—in one piece.

Walter's eyes opened wide. "I *saw* him smash it."

Danny scooped up the pieces from the driveway. He showed Walter a handful of buttons. "It's magic, turkey brain."

Both Danny and Pete were laughing now.

Walter's ears were burning. "Give me my watch back," he said, grabbing it. Walter ran inside.

After dinner that night Walter went straight up to his room and started his pitcher exercises. Twenty pushups and eight pull-ups. Walter had read all about it in Chapter Two—Exercises for Strong Arms. It took strong arms to throw a good fastball.

Danny walked into their room and stood over Walter. "Why're you working up a sweat?"

Walter tried to ignore his brother. Pitchers had to keep their minds on the game. He opened his jar of Tiger Balm. A strong smell filled the room.

Danny sniffed the air and made a face. "Are you stinking up my room with that junk again?"

"It's *my* room too," said Walter.

Danny pointed to a line of tape running along the middle of the floor. "I've already let you use half my room. But *all* the air is mine and you're stinking it up."

Danny grabbed the Tiger Balm out of Walter's hand.

"Give it back!" shouted Walter.

Danny held the jar out of Walter's reach. "Hey, what's this?" Danny picked up *The Pitcher's Guide*.

Walter felt his face getting hot as Danny flipped through it. He grabbed it back.

Danny dropped the Tiger Balm in Walter's lap. "Don't blow it by trying *too* hard, squirt."

Walter sank down on his bed. He felt like a real loser. The game was one day away and he wasn't ready.

"Lighten up, squirt," said Danny. "Baseball's supposed to be fun."

Walter put on his pajamas and crawled into bed with *The Pitcher's Guide*. Danny was a first baseman. He'd never understand. Pitching was serious business.

Mrs. Dodd came in to say good night. "Time to go to sleep." She put Walter's book on his desk.

"Just one more page," begged Walter.

"It can wait," she said, tucking him in. "You've got a big day tomorrow."

"The game isn't until Saturday," said Walter.

"Don't you boys think about anything but baseball?" said Mrs. Dodd. "Parents' Night is tomorrow. Your father and I can't wait. What are you doing for the talent show?"

Walter froze. He had forgotten all about it.

"Is it a surprise?" asked Mrs. Dodd.

Walter nodded quickly.

Mrs. Dodd smiled and turned out the light.

Walter had never felt worse.

As soon as Mrs. Dodd closed the door Danny burst out laughing.

"What's so funny?" said Walter.

"You," said Danny. "You forgot about Parents' Night."

"No, I didn't," said Walter. He was glad the lights were out. His face was bright red.

"Then what are you doing for the talent show?"

"It's a surprise," said Walter. It sounded like a lie even to him.

"Good luck, squirt," said Danny. "You're gonna need it."

Walter knew his brother was right. He reached under the bed for his lucky socks and pulled them on.

Maybe they would work double overnight.

CHAPTER FOUR

Parents' Night

Walter stood in the school hallway watching Mrs. Howard's class get ready for the talent show. He checked his watch. Seven-thirty.

"It feels creepy being here at night," he said to Mike.

"Yeah," said Mike, giving his tie a yank. "I think it's against the law to make kids come to school at night."

Walter nodded. *Mike ought to know,* he thought. His dad was a cop.

"Watch out!" Mike backed up against the wall.

Christy Chung came leaping down the hall in red tights. Yellow paper leaves were pinned to her arms and legs.

"Can you tell what I am?" asked Christy, falling to the ground.

"A dying elephant?" snickered Walter.

Christy frowned. "Very funny. I'm a maple leaf."

"Ignore them, Christy," said Melissa. She was dressed in her cowgirl outfit. "They're just jealous of us."

"Jealous of *these*?" Walter jabbed Melissa's bag of toy horses. "That's a laugh."

"At least I have an act," said Melissa. "Wait until Mrs. Howard finds out you didn't do anything for the talent show."

Everyone looked at Walter.

Walter didn't know what to say. He knelt down to tie his shoe.

"All right, settle down," said Mrs. Howard, joining them in the hall. "Your parents are waiting for the show to begin. Line up in order. We'll start with Mike Lasky."

Walter watched Mike pull out a sheet of

piano music. He felt desperate. "What am I gonna do?" he whispered to Mike.

"Hide in the bathroom until it's over," Mike whispered back. "I'll give you a signal when the coast is clear."

Walter sighed with relief. Maybe it would work. Mike usually had pretty good ideas.

"Next, Melissa Nichols will show her horse collection," said Mrs. Howard. "Then we have Christy's ballet solo."

Christy Chung danced up the line.

"Let's see . . . who's next?" Mrs. Howard searched her clipboard.

Mike leaned out of line and gave Walter the signal.

Walter's heart pounded as he made a dash for the boys' room. He burst through the door and crashed into a boy. He was wearing a long black cape and a top hat.

It was Pete Santos!

"What are you doing here?" grumbled Walter. Pete was the last person he wanted to see.

"Getting my magic act ready." Pete swirled his cape around and held it up in front of his face.

"I am Santos the Magnificent," he said in a deep voice. "Mrs. Howard said I could go on last."

Walter peeked inside Pete's box of tricks.

"What're you doing for the show?" asked Pete.

"Nothing." Walter braced himself for one of Pete's jokes. But Pete didn't say anything. He was busy penciling a thin moustache above his mouth.

"That looks great," said Walter.

Pete handed Walter the pencil. "Try it."

Walter drew a long droopy moustache on his face. He smiled at himself in the mirror.

Pete propped a big cardboard poster up on the sink. It had a drawing of Pete in his top hat and cape holding a magic wand. The poster read:

SANTOS THE MAGNIFICENT

"Nice," said Walter. He touched some gold glitter pasted around the edges. It came off on his fingers.

"Tony helped me," said Pete. Tony Pappas was the best artist in the third grade. Pete loaded the poster into his box of tricks. "Well, gotta go," he said, and swept out the door.

38

Walter walked over to the window and looked outside. The playground was dark. Everything was quiet. He felt all alone. *I'll have to stay in here forever,* he thought.

Suddenly he heard the door open.

Walter turned around.

It was Pete. "Want to be my assistant?" he asked.

Walter looked down at the glitter on his fingers. "I don't know how," he said softly.

"So what?" said Pete, shoving the box of tricks into Walter's arms. "Let's get started. We've got ten minutes before showtime."

Exactly ten minutes later Walter stood beside Pete in front of a roomful of parents.

Pete's poster was propped up on an easel. It read:

SANTOS THE MAGNIFICENT
and his assistant,
WALTER THE WONDERFUL

Mrs. Howard stood up to announce the final act. "Last but not least, Pete Santos and Walter Dodd will end our evening with a magic show."

39

Everyone clapped.

Mr. Dodd gave Walter an A-OK sign from the second row. Mrs. Dodd waved. Walter smiled and waved back. Grandpa Walt was there wearing his Never Sink Nine cap.

"We're on," Pete whispered from behind the curtain. They had hung a sheet between two chairs.

Walter cleared his throat and stepped forward. "Ladies and gentlemen, I have the great pleasure of introducing to you the famous—"

"*World* famous," whispered Pete.

"—the world famous, Santos the Magnificent!"

Pete stepped out from behind the curtain swirling his cape around him. He pointed to Walter with his magic wand. "Meet my able assistant, Walter the Wonderful!"

Walter took a bow. Then he stepped behind the curtain so only his head was showing.

"And now, my friends," said Pete, "I give you the great singer, Walter!"

Walter began singing "Row, Row, Row Your Boat."

40

"Walter is so good he can sing standing on his head," said Pete.

Walter's head went down and his feet came up from behind the curtain.

Walter continued singing!

The audience clapped and cheered.

Suddenly Pete tripped and the curtain fell down. Everyone saw Walter holding his shoes up on his hands!

Walter stared out at the audience. They were all laughing. His face turned bright red. Even Mrs. Howard was laughing. Walter couldn't believe it, but *Pete* was laughing too! Pete didn't even care if his trick went wrong. He was laughing right along with everyone else.

"Whoops!" said Pete. "Well, what do you think I am, a magician?" He twirled around in his cape and faced Walter. "Shall we try another trick?"

Walter nodded nervously. The audience was smiling. They didn't even care if he and Pete had goofed up. They were having fun!

Pete leaned over and stared at Walter's jacket. He shook his head. "You've got a loose thread."

41

Pete took hold of the loose thread and pulled and pulled and pulled. Pete kept backing up until the loose thread stretched across the whole room!

Everyone clapped.

When Pete returned to the front of the room Walter was sitting on a chair. Pete bent over and looked at Walter's shirt. "You have a nice jacket. But that shirt is too tight. And it's really ugly."

Suddenly Pete grabbed Walter's shirt collar and jerked the whole shirt off right over Walter's head!

Walter pretended to look surprised.

Pete dangled Walter's shirt in front of the audience as everyone oohed and aahed.

Walter saw Melissa's eyes open wide in amazement. He smiled. It was fun being part of a magic team.

Pete shoved a box of crayons at Walter. "Colors," he whispered.

Walter nodded and held the box of crayons up for everyone to see. "Santos the Magnificent claims he has the magic power to *smell* colors. Let's give him a test."

Walter turned Pete around. Then he took all the crayons out of the box. He walked up to

Melissa's mother, who was sitting in the front row. "Pick one," said Walter.

Mrs. Nichols picked out a red crayon and held it up high for everyone to see.

Walter put the red crayon in the box and closed it.

"Santos the Magnificent, please turn around and put your hands behind your back," said Walter.

Pete put his hands behind his back. Walter placed the box in Pete's hands.

"Santos the Magnificent will now smell the color," said Walter.

Pete held the closed box up to his nose and sniffed.

"Is it a yellow crayon?" asked Walter in a loud voice so everyone could hear.

Pete shook his head.

"Blue?"

Pete shook his head again.

"Red?"

"Yes," said Pete. "It's a red crayon."

Everyone clapped.

"Awesome!" shouted Otis Hooper, jumping out of his chair.

44

Walter and Pete took a deep bow.

Pete stepped forward. "Now for the greatest trick of all. I'll prove that I have X-ray eyes. I can see what's written on a paper even when it's covered. Who wants to write something?"

Nearly everyone raised a hand. Tony Pappas waved his hand back and forth.

Walter handed Tony a piece of paper and pencil. Tony wrote something on it. "Please fold the paper," said Walter.

Walter took the piece of folded paper to the front of the room and stood on it. "Okay, Santos the Magnificent, what's on the paper?"

"Your big feet!" said Pete.

Everyone laughed as Walter picked up the paper. He unfolded it for everyone to see. In big letters it read

Mrs. Howard stood up. "Please help yourselves to cookies and punch!"

An admiring crowd gathered around Walter and Pete.

"Wow, that shirt trick was great," said Mike. "How'd you do it?"

Walter and Pete pretended to zipper their lips shut.

"Magicians never tell their secrets," said Pete. He smiled at Walter.

Mrs. Howard squeezed Walter's shoulder. "You boys were wonderful," she said.

Walter felt like a movie star. This was the best night of his life.

Melissa Nichols pushed through the crowd. "Your act was a *real* surprise," she said. "It was the best act in the whole show."

"Thanks," said Walter. "Your horse thing was pretty good, too."

Walter found his grandfather over by the cookie table filling paper cups with punch. He handed Walter a cup and two cookies. "Nice job," he said. "Looks like you've found a new friend."

Walter looked over at Pete. He knew if it weren't for Pete he'd still be hiding in the bathroom. "I thought he was just a joker," said Walter.

Grandpa Walt nodded. "Did you know Babe Ruth played jokes all the time too?" he said. "He wasn't just a ballplayer."

Pete stepped up to the table. He took off his top hat and pulled a cookie out of it.

Grandpa Walt clapped and poured him a cup of punch. "You boys make a good team," he said. "Think you can work magic on the Bug Busters at tomorrow's game?"

Walter stared at his grandfather. He had forgotten all about baseball and the Bug Busters. Suddenly he wished he could really do magic. Maybe then he could learn to be a good pitcher before tomorrow's game.

CHAPTER FIVE

Double Trouble

First thing Saturday morning Walter reached under his bed for his lucky socks. He held them up to his face and breathed deeply.

"Mmmmm." At last they were starting to *smell* lucky.

Danny flopped over in bed and sniffed the air. "Are you wearing those cruddy socks again?"

"They're lucky," said Walter, pulling them on. He stuck out his feet and admired the dirty grey color. They used to be blue.

"They stink!" said Danny, reaching under his

pillow. He pulled out his water pistol and pointed it at Walter. "Wash them or else!"

"No!" Walter grabbed his backpack and made a dash for the door. A stream of water hit his back.

"Gotcha!" yelled Danny.

Walter ran outside and got on his bike. He didn't have time for water fights today. He was pitching his first game for the Never Sink Nine. He checked inside his backpack for *The Pitcher's Guide* and pushed off for Diamond Park.

Walter found the Bug Busters warming up on the Babe Ruth field.

"Hey, look!" Robert Decker pointed to Walter. "It's the glass-arm pitcher!"

Walter's ears burned. "What makes you think you're so great?"

"Watch this," said Robert. He wound up and fired a fastball into his twin brother's mitt.

The ball flew by so fast Walter barely saw it.

The Decker twins grinned at Walter. They each had a front tooth missing.

"You call that fast?" Walter pretended to laugh, but he was so nervous it sounded more like a cough.

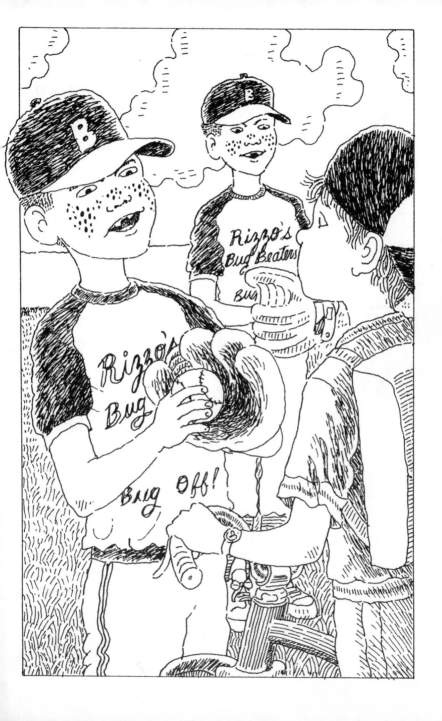

"What's wrong?" teased Robert. "Got a *fly* ball in your throat?"

Walter hurried into the dugout and got out *The Pitcher's Guide*. It had to have a chapter to help him.

The Never Sink Nine started filling the dugout. Melissa set her backpack down next to Walter and pulled out her mitt. "Wanna throw some?" she asked.

"Sure," said Walter. He looked across the field and saw the Decker twins. "Um, maybe later," he mumbled uncertainly.

Melissa shrugged and cantered onto the field. The Bug Busters and the Never Sink Nine were warming up, side by side.

"Hi there, slugger."

Walter looked up from his book at Grandpa Walt.

Grandpa Walt lifted *The Pitcher's Guide* from Walter's hands. "You don't need this, sport," he said, sitting down next to Walter.

Walter nodded his head toward the Decker twins. "They're a lot better than me. Melissa's better, too."

Grandpa Walt gave Walter a hug. "Don't

think about how the others play," he said. "Play ball your own way." He looked around the dugout. "Do you know where Tony is?"

Walter shook his head.

"It's not like him not to show up," said Grandpa Walt. Even though Tony had a broken leg and couldn't play, he came to every game. He always took roll call.

Mike came running into the dugout. "We're up at bat first!" he said, swinging an imaginary bat through the air. Since Billy Baskin moved away Mike was the clean-up batter. He was the best hitter on the team.

Grandpa Walt went over the batting lineup. "Let's start off with our new teammate, Pete Santos." Grandpa Walt looked up. "Is Pete here?"

"Here," came a voice from the corner.

Pete was standing in a corner of the dugout. He wasn't cracking jokes or playing magic tricks. He wasn't even smiling. He was looking down at his bat. He wished they had done some batting at practice.

"Batter up!" shouted one of the Decker twins from the pitcher's mound.

Pete dragged a bat over to home plate.

53

"You can do it!" shouted Grandpa Walt.

Pete forced a smile. He lifted the bat and waited for the first pitch.

The first two balls whizzed past.

Pete swung late on both.

"What's the matter?" shouted Robert Decker from the pitcher's mound. "Got a hole in your bat?"

"Strike three!" shouted the umpire as the last ball went over the plate.

Pete didn't even take a swing.

"Boy, he sure is nervous," Mike said to Walter. "Did you see his legs shake? Guess it's tough being the new kid."

Walter had more important things to think about. He closed his eyes and tried to remember the signal for a fastball.

The Never Sink Nine didn't get one hit off the Decker twins for the first three innings. At the bottom of the fourth inning Robert handed the ball to Walter. "It's all yours."

Walter walked slowly to the mound. He rubbed his Babe Ruth watch for luck and pulled up his lucky socks. But he still felt like a loser.

Walter walked the first two hitters.

"You need a pitcher, not a glass of water!" chanted the Bug Busters.

Walter was feeling worse and worse.

"Ba-a-a-a-a! Ba-a-a-a-a!" Even Homer was laughing at him.

The Never Sink Nine mascot was grazing over by the Bug Busters' dugout. Homer sniffed the jars of bugs lined up on the dugout ledge. They were the Bug Busters' mascots.

One of the Decker twins shoved Homer away with a baseball bat.

Pete ran in fast from first base. "Leave Homer alone!" he shouted.

"Keep your goat away from our mascots!" yelled Richard Decker.

"Yeah!" yelled Robert.

Homer lowered his head. One by one, he butted the jars off the ledge. Glass crashed to the ground. Ants and grasshoppers swarmed all over the Bug Busters' dugout. Their team jumped up and down, swatting off their mascots.

"Good old Homer," said Pete. He brushed a few ants off Homer's Never Sink Nine team cap.

"Batter up!" Walter said loudly, slapping the ball into his mitt. He tried not to laugh.

Robert Decker was up to bat next.

Walter thought of Babe Ruth. He wound up and threw the ball right over home plate.

"Strike one!" yelled the umpire.

Robert Decker was too busy shaking ants off his pants leg to swing.

"What's wrong?" said Walter. "Got ants in your pants?"

Robert swung wildly at the next two balls.

"Strike three!" said the umpire. "You're out!"

The Bug Busters' coach stalked over to Grandpa Walt. "Time-out!" he yelled. "We've got to get these ants out of our uniforms. Everyone change in the equipment shed!"

The Bug Busters all charged across the field to the equipment shed. They were in such a hurry that Robert and Richard Decker tumbled on top of each other.

"Look!" Walter pointed to the twins. "It's a double Decker!"

Pete started laughing. "Double Decker," he said. "That's a good one, Walter."

Walter smiled. He was glad Pete wasn't scared anymore. He wasn't scared either. Baseball was too much fun to be scared about.

Soon it was the top of the sixth inning and the Never Sink Nine was behind, four to three. Pete was on second base with two out.

"Who's up next?" asked Walter. He was used to Tony calling out the batting order.

Grandpa Walt checked his clipboard. "Mike Lasky."

Mike didn't have to hear his name called twice. He was always eager to hit. Mike slipped on his batting gloves and grabbed his bat. He started for the plate.

"Hey, Mike," said Otis. "If you hit Pete home you'll tie the game."

"Yeah," said Melissa. "Hit Pete home."

Mike swallowed hard. "Okay."

Jenny tugged on Walter's sleeve. She pointed toward Pete on second base. "What's Pete doing?" she asked.

Walter looked up. Pete was squeezing the second baseman's nose. Pennies dropped to the ground. The Never Sink Nine was depending on Pete and he was doing magic tricks!

"Pete!" shouted Walter.

Pete waved at Walter and went back to his penny trick.

Homer nudged Walter and licked his hand. Walter hid his face in Homer's fur. "I can't look."

Mike let the first two balls go by. Strikes.

"What's he waiting for?" said Otis. "An invitation?"

Walter looked up. He knew Mike was just waiting for the right ball. He watched Mike dig in and take a couple of practice swings. He was ready.

Ting!

Mike hammered a grounder past the pitcher straight to second base! The second baseman was busy trying Pete's penny trick. The ball bounced past him into the outfield.

Pete had rounded third and was on his way home.

"Run, Pete, run!" screamed Walter.

"Come on!" The Never Sink Nine cheered on their teammate.

One of the Bug Busters finally caught up with the ball and threw it in to third. The third baseman spun around and whipped it toward home plate.

"Slide!" shouted Grandpa Walt.

"Slide!" yelled the Never Sink Nine.

Pete slid into home on his side, feet first. His sneakers scraped across the ground. A cloud of dust hid everything.

Walter leaned out to hear the call. The umpire raised his head above the dust. Walter held his breath.

"Safe!"

The Never Sink Nine raced over to Pete. Walter and Mike helped him to his feet.

"How'd you do it?" asked Walter.

Pete wiped the dust from his eyes. He smiled and pulled a penny from Walter's ear. "Magic."

Pete's run tied the score four to four. After that, Katie Kessler struck out. It was the bottom of the last inning and the Bug Busters were up at bat.

Walter took the mound. He ground the ball into his mitt and looked around the diamond. Only one person could keep the Bug Busters from scoring now.

It was up to him.

CHAPTER SIX

All-Star Homer

Things didn't look good for the Never Sink Nine. It was the bottom of the sixth inning with two outs and the bases loaded. Walter had walked three players and struck out two. The Bug Busters needed only one run to win.

Walter pulled up his lucky socks and waited for the next batter.

Richard Decker strutted up to home plate and took a practice swing. "I'm ready, Glass Arm," he yelled at Walter.

Walter ignored him. He slapped the ball into his mitt and took a quick check around the field.

All the positions were covered. Homer was grazing quietly on the sidelines near right field next to Jenny.

Walter watched Otis for the signal.

Otis pointed two fingers down.

A fastball.

Walter's arm was tired but he nodded. Melissa had pitched three innings and so would he. Walter wound up and fired a fastball.

Crack!

A fly ball to right field!

"Get it, Jenny!" shouted Walter.

Jenny raised her mitt in the air and closed her eyes.

The Bug Busters were running bases. They started crossing home plate, one by one.

Walter's heart sank with the fly ball over right field. Jenny was nowhere near it.

Homer looked up and spotted the ball. The goat took a flying leap into the air and caught the ball squarely in his mouth!

"They're out!" shouted Walter, tossing his mitt in the air. "It's a tie!"

Jenny opened her eyes and saw Homer with the ball in his mouth. She threw her arms around the goat's furry neck. "Thank you, Homer."

The Decker twins stomped over to the umpire. "We won," they grumbled. "Goats can't play."

The Never Sink Nine gathered around Homer. Everyone was patting him and feeding him grass. Homer wagged his short tail and butted them gently with his head.

"I knew he could do it," said Pete, proudly. "He's loved baseball since he was a kid."

Grandpa Walt walked toward them across the field. "Hold on, everyone. I've got bad news. Homer's catch is disqualified."

Everyone groaned.

Grandpa Walt held his hand up to silence them. "Much as we love Homer, he's a goat, not a real team player."

Homer bleated sadly. "Ba-a-a-a-a."

Grandpa Walt patted Homer. "Sorry, old boy."

No one said a word.

"Let's head over to the Pizza Palace," said Grandpa Walt.

The team piled into Grandpa Walt's old station wagon. No one felt like asking whose turn it was to choose the pizza toppings.

"I forgot to tell you something," said Grandpa Walt. "Because of the unusual circumstances the Bug Busters' coach suggested a rematch next week."

Walter and Mike smacked their hands together in a high-five. "All right!" said Walter.

"We'll beat 'em next time," said Mike.

"Yeah," said Melissa. "They won't forget us."

When they got to the Pizza Palace, Tony Pappas was standing out front waiting.

"Why weren't you at the game?" asked Walter.

Tony and Grandpa Walt smiled at each other. "It's a surprise," said Tony. "Notice anything different?"

"What?" asked Mike.

Melissa stared at Tony's leg—the one that was broken. "His cast is gone!"

Tony nodded. "The doctor took it off this morning. She said I could start playing ball pretty soon."

"Great," said Walter. "Now you won't have to sit around drawing pictures."

Tony pulled a small drawing pad out of his pocket. A pencil rested behind one ear. "Oh, I'll always draw," he said.

"Let's eat!" said Pete, leading the way inside. "Coach says it's my turn to choose."

Pete chose pizza with extra cheese, red peppers, and meatballs.

Everyone was eating and filling Tony in on the game—everyone but Jenny.

"What's wrong, Jen?" asked Pete. "Don't you like the pizza I picked?"

Jenny nodded and took a small bite. She tugged at one of her pigtails. "I never catch any balls. I'm always doing stuff wrong."

Pete shook his head. "That's impossible. You can't do anything wrong. Know why?"

Jenny shook her head.

"Because you're the *right* fielder." Pete reached behind Jenny's ear and pulled out a penny. He gave it to her.

"It's a lucky penny," said Jenny, holding it tight in one hand. "I'm going to catch balls from now on." She took a big bite of pizza.

After everyone had finished their pizza Grandpa Walt treated the team to double-decker ice cream cones.

"This is what we'll do to the Decker twins," said Walter, taking a big bite. "Get it?" he asked everyone.

Everyone took big bites and ate up the competition.

Later that night at home Walter rolled his lucky socks into a ball and put them in his mitt. He stuffed the mitt under his pillow.

Danny got into bed and turned out the light. "Our team beat the stuffing out of the Landslides today. How was your game, squirt?"

"Fun," said Walter. He didn't bother to say they had lost. It didn't seem to matter.

Walter grabbed *The Pitcher's Guide* and a flashlight off the floor. He made a tent out of his covers and turned on the flashlight.

He had one whole chapter left. Walter skipped to the last paragraph.

It doesn't matter what position you play on a team

or how many balls you hit. Just remember to have fun. That is what baseball is all about.

Walter closed the book and leaned back on his pillow.

Why did they always save the best part for last?

Tomorrow he would ask Grandpa Walt.

About the Author

GIBBS DAVIS was born in Milwaukee, Wisconsin, graduated from the University of California at Berkeley, and lives in New York City. Her first novel, *Maud Flies Solo,* is also a Bantam Skylark book. She has published *Swann Song,* a young adult novel, with Avon Books. *Walter's Lucky Socks, Major-League Melissa, Slugger Mike,* and *Pete the Magnificent* are part of The Never Sink Nine series for First Skylark.

About the Illustrator

GEORGE ULRICH was born in Morristown, New Jersey, and received his Bachelor of Fine Arts degree from Syracuse University. He has illustrated several Bantam Skylark books, including *Make Four Million Dollars by Next Thursday!* by Stephen Manes and *The Amazing Adventure of Me, Myself, and I* by Jovial Bob Stine. He lives in Marblehead, Massachusetts, with his wife and two sons.

A BANTAM FIRST SKYLARK

ERRATA

Pete's magic tricks, which were promised to you on the back cover of this book, have mysteriously disappeared! Here they are:

PETE THE MAGNIFICENT'S MAGIC TRICKS

Off with the Shirt Trick

Walter's shirt appears to be buttoned as usual under his jacket, but the cuffs and front are unbuttoned. Walter has draped the loose shirt over himself with only the neck showing. When you do this trick make sure the loose sleeves don't show. All Pete had to do was grab Walter's collar and jerk the shirt over Walter's head. The clip-on tie was left unhooked in the back.

Loose Thread Trick

Pete threaded a needle onto thread still attached to the spool. The spool was put into Walter's jacket pocket. The thread was run through a buttonhole in the jacket. The needle was then taken away so it looked like a loose thread.

I Can Smell Colors Trick

When Pete held the box behind him he stuck his finger in and scratched the mystery crayon with his thumbnail. When Pete held the box to his nose he could see the color on his thumbnail.

Watch Trick

Pete only pretended to pass the watch to his right hand. He realy kept it in his left hand. He had the buttons ready to throw down in his right hand.